177306

D1635648

F

A Letter
To Granny

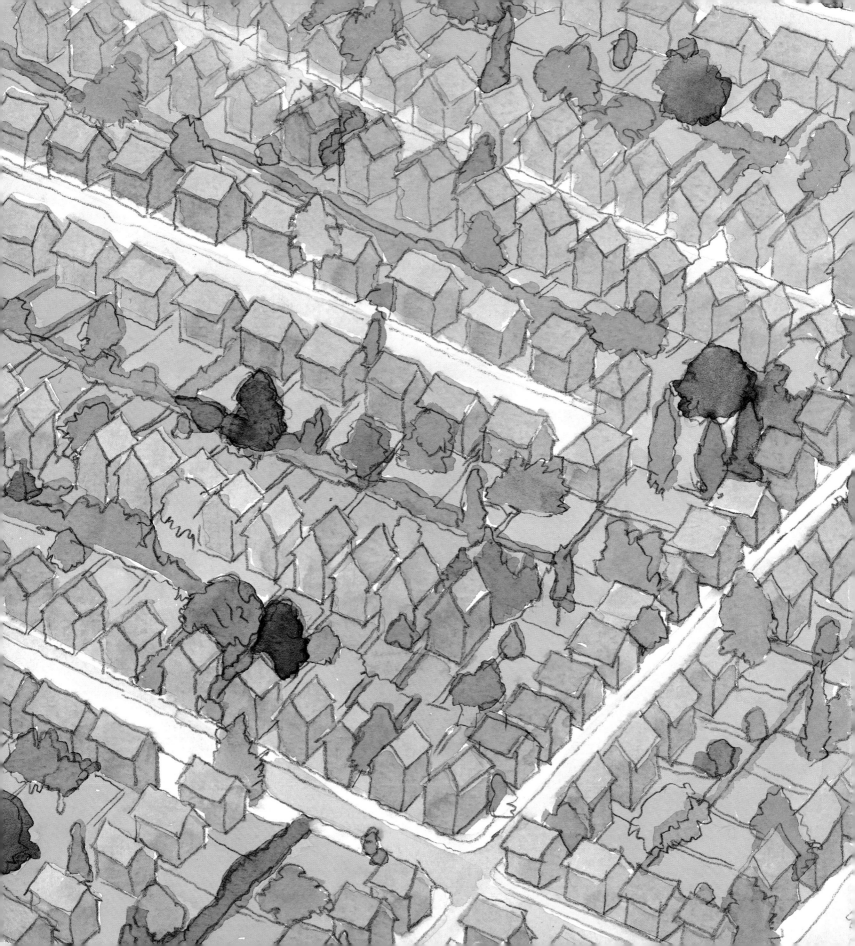

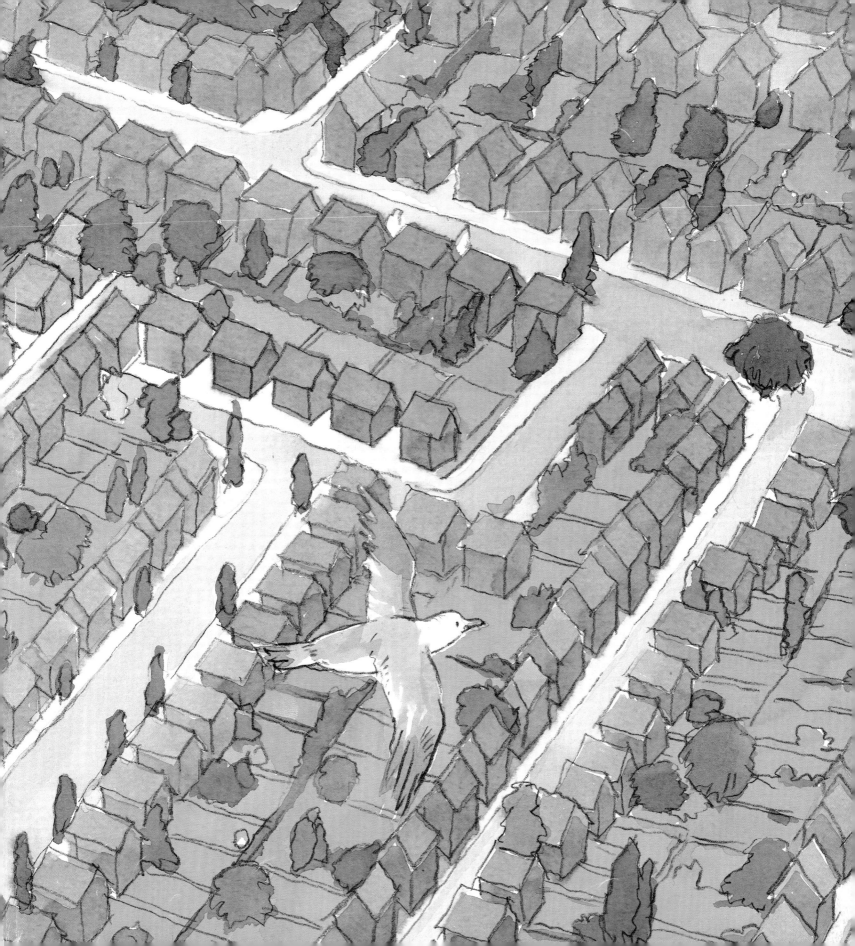

For Laura and Clara – PR

A Red Fox Book

Published by Random House Children's Books
20 Vauxhall Bridge Road, London SW1V 2SA

A division of Random House UK Ltd
London Melbourne Sydney Auckland
Johannesburg and agencies throughout the world

Copyright © text Paul Rogers 1994
Copyright © illustrations John Prater 1994

3 5 7 9 10 8 6 4 2

First published in Great Britain by
The Bodley Head Children's Books 1994

Red Fox edition 1996

This book is sold subject to the condition that it shall not, by way of
trade or otherwise, be lent, resold, hired out, or otherwise circulated
without the publisher's prior consent in any form of binding or cover
other than that in which it is published and without a similar condition
including this condition being imposed on the subsequent purchaser.

The right of Paul Rogers and John Prater to be identified as the author
and illustrator of this work has been asserted by them in accordance with
the Copyright, Designs and Patents Act, 1988.

Printed in Hong Kong

RANDOM HOUSE UK Limited Reg. No. 954009

ISBN 0 09 928881 8

A LETTER
TO GRANNY

Paul Rogers · John Prater

Red Fox

FALKIRK COUNCIL
LIBRARY SUPPORT
FOR SCHOOLS

Lucy lay in her bed, in her room, in her house, in her street, and thought of the whole town spread out around her.

She fell asleep listening to night noises – distant cars and dogs barking into the dark – and thinking about tomorrow, when Granny would come.

The moment she woke, she knew
something was different. Where had all
the houses gone? The streets? The town?
From her window she could see nothing
but sea!

She ran out of the house, barefoot
on to the sand – past the garden,
past the garage, past the front door, under
her own bedroom window.

'Breakfast's ready!' Mum called.

Lucy climbed back up the cliff, leaving
a necklace of footprints around the island.

'The postman's late,' said Dad.

'I expect the traffic's bad,' said Mum.

'I'm going out to watch the whales,'
said Lucy.

That's where my school used to be, she thought, over there. This is where the road was. She picked up a starfish. 'And there,' she laughed, as two crabs scuttled away, 'that's where Mr and Mrs Horner lived.'

At lunchtime, Lucy told Mum and Dad all about the rock pools, the fish and the sea. But they didn't seem to be listening.

During pudding there was a knock at the door.
'I'll go!' Lucy said.

An enormous liner was anchored off the front garden. On the step stood its captain. 'Pardon me,' he said. 'I think we're lost. I can't work out where I am.'

'This is 101 Acacia Road,' said Lucy.

'Ah, thank you,' said the captain. 'Sorry to trouble you.'

After lunch Lucy's parents worked in the garden.
'Look at these lupins!' complained Mum.

'Look at those dolphins!' called Lucy from the beach.

Suddenly she remembered Granny.
How ever would she get here now?
Someone would have to tell her!
At her toes Lucy saw an old bottle.
She hurried indoors for pen and
paper and wrote:

Dear Granny,
I can't wait to see you.
Our new address is
101 Acacia Road Island.
Please come soon.
Love from Lucy

Then rolling the message up, she
slipped it into the bottle and pushed
it out to sea.

That was when Lucy felt the first drops of rain. The sky grew dark, the sea grew wild, and soon Lucy was hurrying to the house for shelter. From the window she watched the storm.

Now Granny will never make it, she thought.

Then, way out in the distance, she spotted a small boat. One moment it was riding a giant wave, the next it was lost from sight. But gradually it grew bigger and bigger until Lucy could make out her Granny, waving.

'Hello Granny!' she called, running to the water's edge as the rain stopped. Together they climbed the path to the house.

'You look a bit wet,' said Dad. 'Did you have to wait for the bus?'

After tea, Lucy took Granny on a tour of the island. She showed
her the crabs and gulls, the rock pools and starfish.

'Look,' said Granny, 'I've something for you. Hold it to your ear.
What do you hear?'

So Lucy pressed the warm-coloured, soft-looking, cold, hard shell
to her ear. And in it she heard the sound of the sea.

Then she sat on Granny's lap, on the deckchair, on the beach, on the island, and together they watched the ripe sun going down.

When it was time for Granny to go, Lucy waved her
goodbye from the gate. She watched her climbing into
the boat and sailing slowly, slowly away.

'Time for bed,' said Dad.

'I expect Granny will steer by the stars,' said Lucy.

That night, Lucy fell asleep listening to the
sighing of the sea and dreaming all about . . .

. . . tomorrow.

FALKIRK COUNCIL
LIBRARY SUPPORT
FOR SCHOOLS

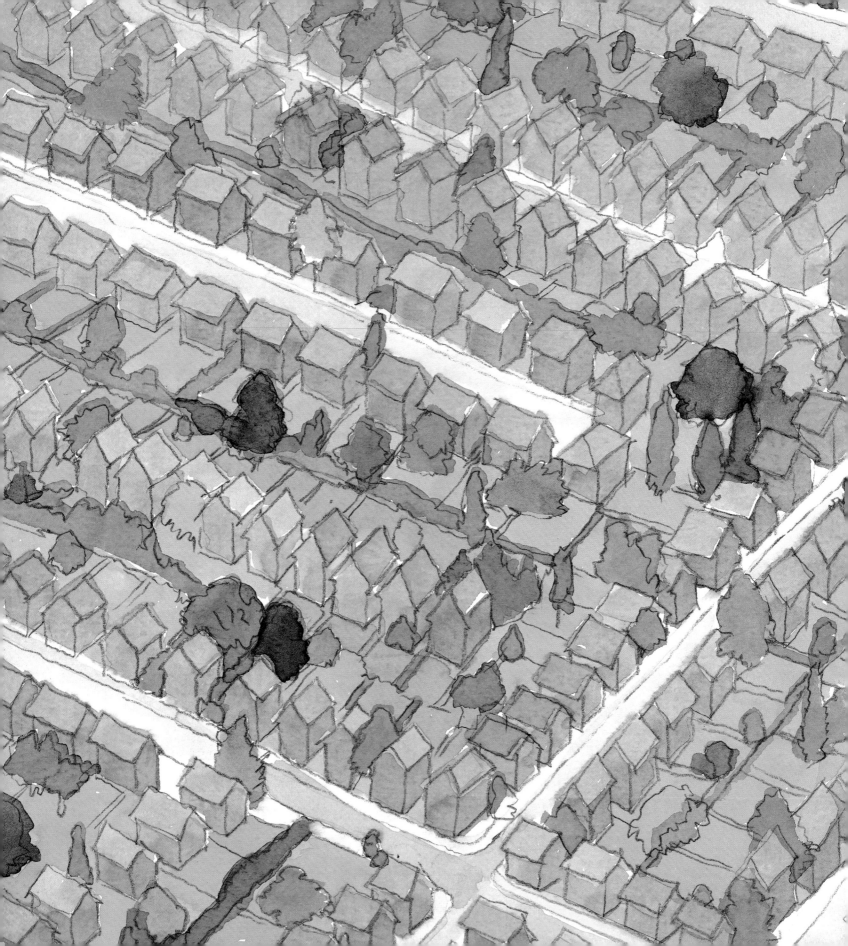

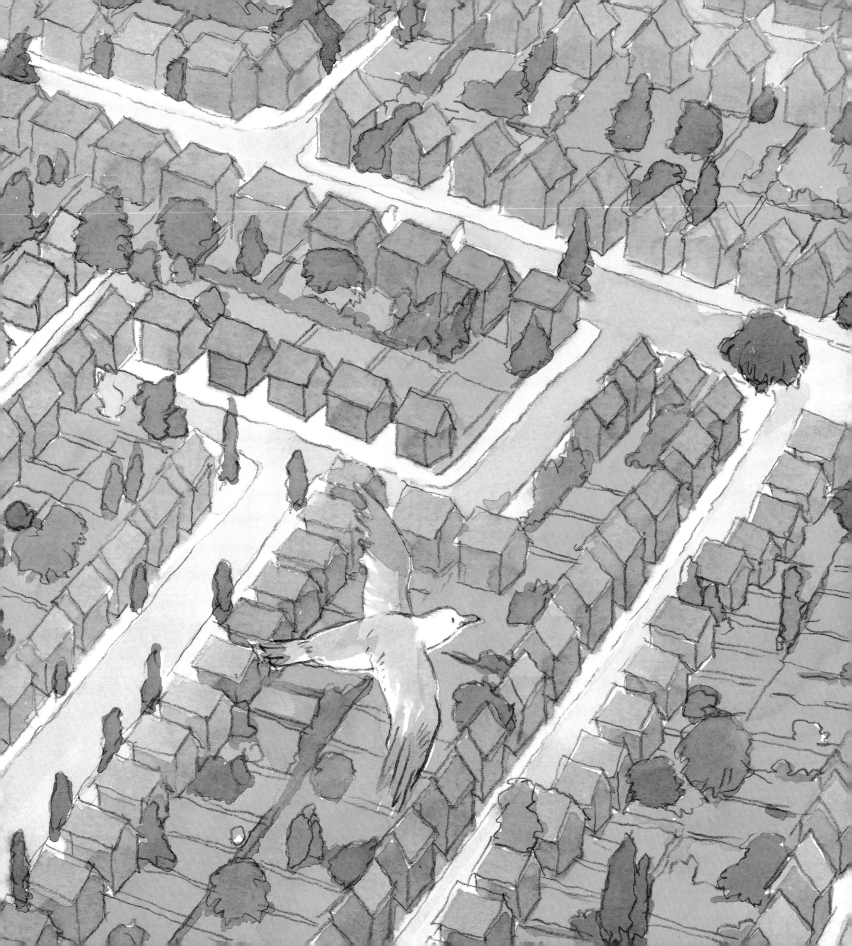

Some bestselling Red Fox picture books

THE BIG ALFIE AND ANNIE ROSE STORYBOOK
by Shirley Hughes
OLD BEAR
by Jane Hissey
OI! GET OFF OUR TRAIN
by John Burningham
DON'T DO THAT!
by Tony Ross
NOT NOW, BERNARD
by David McKee
ALL JOIN IN
by Quentin Blake
THE WHALES' SONG
by Gary Blythe and Dyan Sheldon
JESUS' CHRISTMAS PARTY
by Nicholas Allan
THE PATCHWORK CAT
by Nicola Bayley and William Mayne
MATILDA
by Hilaire Belloc and Posy Simmonds
WILLY AND HUGH
by Anthony Browne
THE WINTER HEDGEHOG
by Ann and Reg Cartwright
A DARK, DARK TALE
by Ruth Brown
HARRY, THE DIRTY DOG
by Gene Zion and Margaret Bloy Graham
DR XARGLE'S BOOK OF EARTHLETS
by Jeanne Willis and Tony Ross
WHERE'S THE BABY?
by Pat Hutchins